The White Horse

and other horse stories

Compiled by Vic Parker

Miles Kelly

First published in 2014 by Miles Kelly Publishing Ltd
Harding's Barn, Bardfield End Green, Thaxted, Essex, CM6 3PX, UK

2 4 6 8 10 9 7 5 3 1

Publishing Director Belinda Gallagher
Creative Director Jo Cowan
Editorial Director Rosie Neave
Senior Editor Claire Philip
Designer Rob Hale
Production Manager Elizabeth Collins
Reprographics Stephan Davis, Jennifer Hunt, Thom Allaway

ISBN 978-1-78209-458-6

Printed in China

British Library Cataloguing-in-Publication Data
A catalogue record for this book is available from the British Library

ACKNOWLEDGEMENTS
The publishers would like to thank the following artists who have contributed to this book:
Advocate Art: Simon Mendez (Cover)
The Bright Agency: Mélanie Florian, Kirsteen Harris-Jones (inc. borders)

Made with paper from a sustainable forest

www.mileskelly.net
info@mileskelly.net

Contents

The Lightning Horse and the Prince of Persia

By James Baldwin

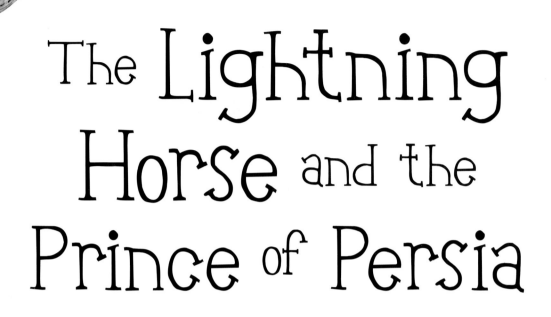

This is a retelling of a folktale from Persia (modern-day Iran). It was first written down by a poet called Ferdowsi, around one thousand years ago in the 'Shanameh', or 'Book of Kings', a mixture of Persian mythology and history dating back to the beginning of the world.

WHEN RUSTEM was still a young man, the news came that a vast army of enemies had come down from the north and were threatening to cross into Persia. Rustem begged his father, a prince, to let

him lead a band of warriors against the
invaders. These words pleased his father,
who at once sent out a proclamation into
all the provinces, commanding that on the
first day of the Festival of Roses all the best
horses should be brought to Zaboulistan so
that Rustem could choose one of them to
be his battle steed. The owner of the one
that was selected would be rewarded with
gold, but if anyone should hide a good
horse, he would be punished without mercy.

On the appointed day, the most famous
horse breeders from across all Persia had
assembled their finest horses at Zaboulistan.
Even more horses had been brought in by
common folk. Everyone had brought the
best that he had, and the world had never

seen a more wonderful collection of steeds.

At an early hour in the morning, Prince Zal and young Rustem took up position outside the city gate in a covered pavilion. One by one the horses were led before them. All were swift and strong, and many had been bred especially for Rustem to use one day. But none of them satisfied the young prince.

After hours had passed, the very last horses were presented by some traders from Kabul. But Rustem's eyes moved from the steeds in front of him to another couple of horses further off.

"Whose is that mare over there?" asked Rustem. "And whose is the colt that stays so close to her?"

"We do not know," answered the traders. "But they have followed us all the way from the Afghan valleys, and we have been unable to capture them. We have heard it said, however, that men call the colt Rakush, or Lightning. His mother will let no one near."

The colt gleamed like burnished gold, its chest and shoulders were like those of a lion, and its eyes beamed with the fire of intelligence.

Snatching a noose from the hands of a

herdsman, Rustem ran quickly forwards and threw it over the animal's head. Then followed a terrible battle with its mother but in the end Rustem was the winner. The young prince leaped upon Rakush's back and the golden steed bore him over the plains. They raced back to the city gate. "This is the horse that I choose," he told his father. "Let us give the traders their reward."

"No," answered the men. "Have him with our blessing and save the lands of Iran – for, seated upon Rakush, no enemy will be able to stand before you."

Their words proved true. For Rustem and Rakush led an attack that beat back the invaders – which was only the first bold, brave feat of many.

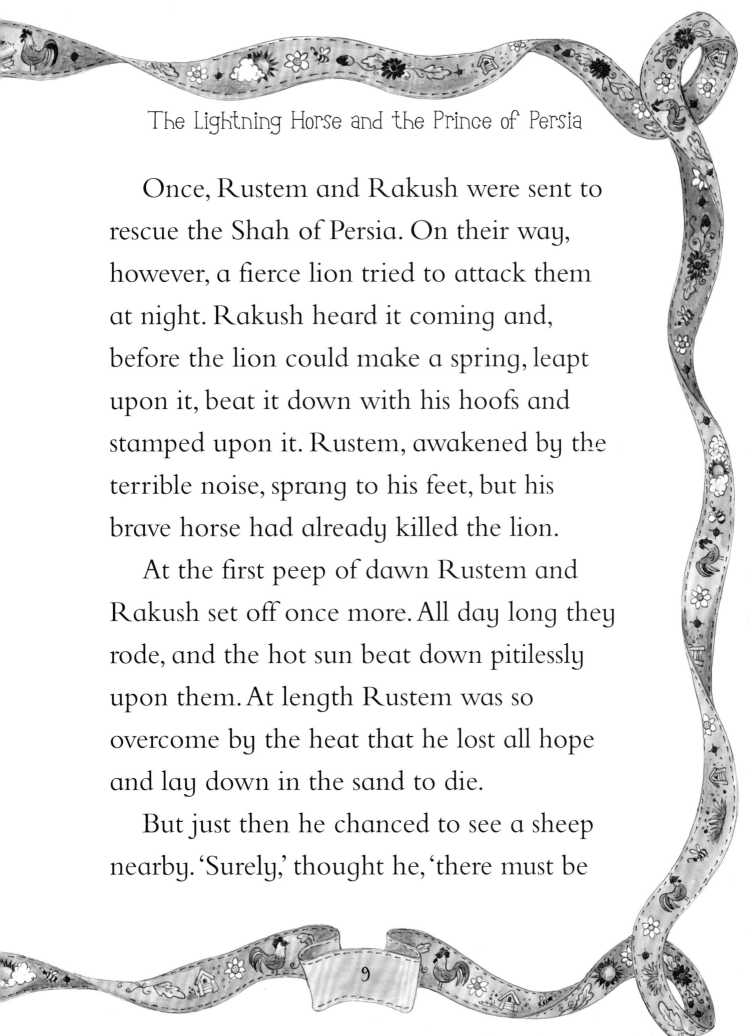

Once, Rustem and Rakush were sent to rescue the Shah of Persia. On their way, however, a fierce lion tried to attack them at night. Rakush heard it coming and, before the lion could make a spring, leapt upon it, beat it down with his hoofs and stamped upon it. Rustem, awakened by the terrible noise, sprang to his feet, but his brave horse had already killed the lion.

At the first peep of dawn Rustem and Rakush set off once more. All day long they rode, and the hot sun beat down pitilessly upon them. At length Rustem was so overcome by the heat that he lost all hope and lay down in the sand to die.

But just then he chanced to see a sheep nearby. 'Surely,' thought he, 'there must be water not far away, or this animal could not be here.' The hope gave him new courage and, remounting Rakush, he urged him forwards. They soon found a little brook. Man and beast drank their fill.

When the sun had set Rustem lay down to sleep while Rakush quietly grazed. All was well until near midnight, when a fierce dragon that lived in the valley came out of its den. It was astonished to see the two.

The dragon was ready to destroy them with its poisonous breath when Rakush, seeing the danger, neighed frantically to awaken his master. Rustem sprang up quickly and seized his sword. The dragon leaped upon Rustem and wrapped itself about him, and would surely have crushed

him to death had not Rakush come to the rescue. The horse used his teeth to seize the dragon from behind and, as it turned to defend itself, Rustem's arm was freed so that he could use his sword. With one mighty stroke he cut off the dragon's head, and the vile serpent of the desert was no more.

Then Rustem praised Rakush highly for his great courage. He carefully washed his gallant horse in the stream, and groomed Rakush until the break of day, and when the sun arose they set out on another day's journey across the burning sands.

Needless to say, Rustem and Rakush triumphed over every peril they met on their way, despite the dangers that befell them in the land of the magicians and in

the country of darkness, where there was no light of sun or stars, and where they were guided by Rakush's instinct alone.

Eventually they arrived in Mazinderan and, after meeting innumerable dangers, delivered the Shah from his dungeon and returned him safely home.

In all the East there was no hero that could be likened unto Rustem, and never a horse that could in any way be compared with Rakush. Many years passed by – years of peace and years of war – and many Shahs sat upon the throne of Iran, but the real power was in the hands of Rustem of Zaboulistan.

And although he lived to a great age, and Rakush was so very, very old that he

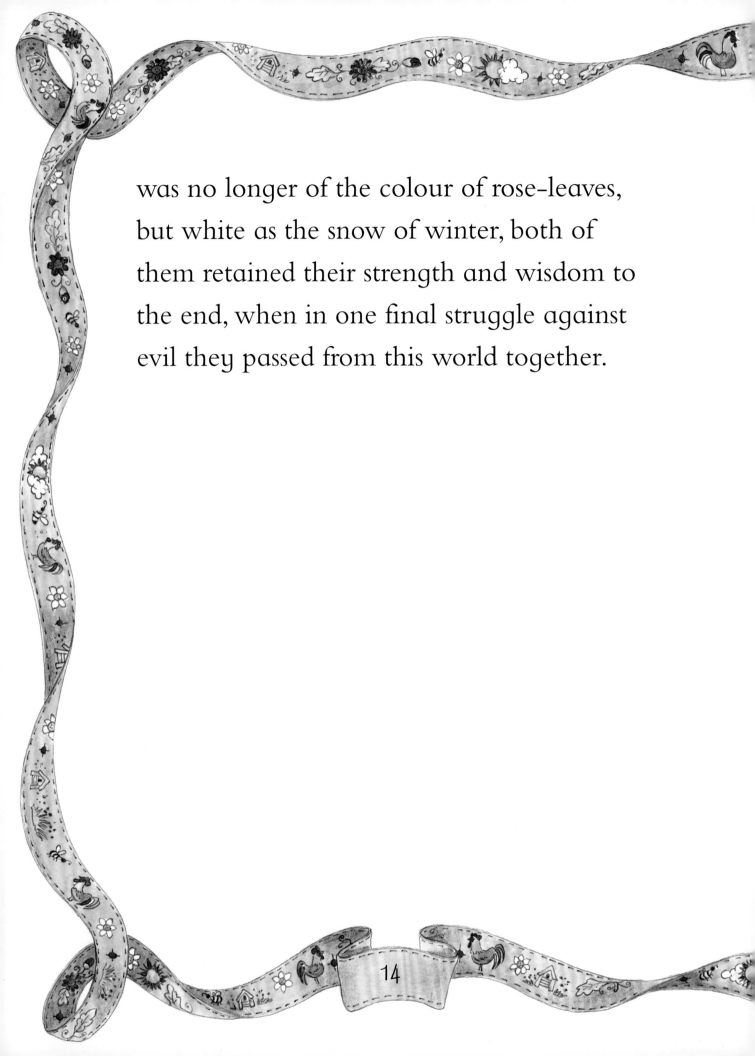

was no longer of the colour of rose-leaves, but white as the snow of winter, both of them retained their strength and wisdom to the end, when in one final struggle against evil they passed from this world together.

The White Horse

By E Nesbit

Edith Nesbit lived in the English county of Kent for around twenty years. The symbol for Kent has been a white horse for over one thousand years. It is often referred to as Invicta, which means unbeaten.

ONCE UPON A TIME, there lived a simple woodcutter's son called Diggory. When a distant uncle sent Diggory the present of a horse, he said goodbye to his father and set out to seek his fortune. He christened the horse 'Invicta'. It was white, with a red saddle and bridle fit for a king, and all the village turned out to see him go.

Diggory rode to the windmill at the edge of the village, then stopped. For the miller's daughter, Joyce, came running up to him. "Take me with you," the pretty girl begged, earnestly. "I can ride behind you on your big horse."

But Diggory said, "No. Why, girls can't go to seek their fortunes. You'd only be in my way! Wish me luck."

So he rode on and she watched him go, her eyes brimming with tears.

Diggory rode on, and on. He rode through the dewy evening, and through the cool black night, and into the fresh-scented dawn. And when it was morning, Diggory felt very thin and empty, and he remembered that he had eaten nothing since dinner-time yesterday.

He rode on and on, and after a time came to a red brick wall, very strong and stout. Invicta was tall, so by standing up in his stirrups, Diggory could see over it. On the other side was an orchard of apple trees, all heavy with red and green fruits.

Diggory stood up on the broad saddle and jumped! In the next moment, he had hauled himself over the wall and dropped down into the orchard. For he was so hungry, he had made up his mind to take some apples.

Diggory climbed the tree with the fattest, rosiest apples. He had just settled himself

astride a convenient bough when he heard a voice say, "Hi! You up there!"

Looking down, he saw an old man looking up spitefully.

"Apple-stealing's punished severely in these parts," he stated, narrowing his eyes. "Besides, did you know that this is an enchanted orchard? You can't just go away as freely as you came in. Why, you can't even get out of that tree…"

To Diggory's horror, he discovered that the old man was right. He could move all about the tree from branch to branch – but suddenly he seemed to be upside down. If he jumped off, he would fall up into the sky – and keep falling upwards forever… So he held tight and looked at the old man.

Then the old man said, "Throw me those ten big apples," and he pointed to some apples nearest the top of the tree, "and I'll let you go out by the Apple Door that no one but me has the key to."

"Why don't you pick them yourself?" Diggory asked.

"I'm too old. Come, is it a bargain?"

"I don't know," said the boy, "there are lots of apples you can reach without climbing. Why do you want these ones?"

As he spoke, he picked one of the apples, threw it up and caught it. I say up, but it was down instead, because of the apple-tree being so very much enchanted.

"Oh, don't drop it!" the old man squeaked. "Throw it down to me, you nasty smock-frocked son of a speckled toad!"

Diggory's blood boiled at hearing his father called a toad.

"Take that!" cried he, aiming the apple at the old man's head. "I wish I could get out of this tree."

The apple hit the old man's head and bounced onto the grass, and the moment that apple touched the ground Diggory found that he could get out of the tree.

"So," he said, "are these wish-apples?"

"No, no, no!" shrieked the old man so earnestly that Diggory knew he was lying.

"I've just disenchanted you, that's all, because I'm a nice kind old man really."

"I wish you'd speak the truth," said Diggory, and with that he picked the second apple and threw it.

Then the old man couldn't help himself. "I am a wicked magician," he had to confess. "I never did anything useful with my magic. The apple trees in this orchard are people that I enchanted. There's only one way out of this place and I don't mean to show it you."

"It's a pity you're so wicked," said Diggory. "I wish you were good."

He threw down another apple and instantly the magician became so good that he could do nothing but sit down and cry.

Diggory was no longer afraid of him, so he gathered the apples that were left and came down the tree.

Then Diggory made three wishes. First, he asked for the old man to be happy as well as good. Then he wished for the apple trees to be disenchanted – and they were.

The White Horse

The orchard was full of kings and princesses, and swineherds and goosegirls, and every kind of person you can or can't think of. The third wish showed Diggory the secret Apple Door. He went out through it and found his good white horse, who had been eating grass very happily all the time. So Invicta was not hungry, but Diggory was, and, in fact, he was so hungry that he had to use a wish-apple to get his supper.

After he had eaten, Diggory rode on anxiously, arranging what wishes he should have with the rest of the apples, but in the dusk he missed his way, plunged into a river and was nearly drowned, while poor white Invicta was quite carried away.

Having clambered onto the bank,

Diggory took off his shirt to wring the water out and as he did so he said, "I wish I had my good white horse again."

And as he said it all the apples but one tumbled out of his shirt onto the ground, and he heard soft neighings and stampings around him in the dark. When the moon rose he saw that he had had his wish – his good white horse was back again. But as he had dropped eight apples, he had his good white horse back eight times – he had now eight good white horses.

"Well, eight horses are even better than one!" he said, and when he had tethered the horses he went to sleep, for he felt strangely feeble and tired.

In the morning he woke with pains in

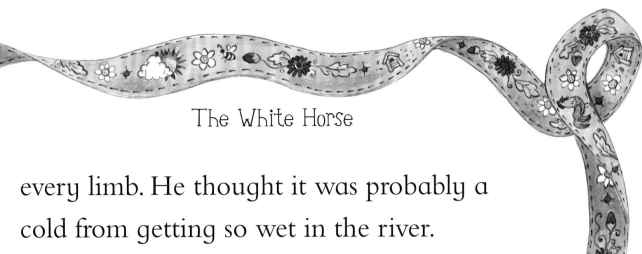

every limb. He thought it was probably a cold from getting so wet in the river. Diggory tied seven of the horses together and led them, riding on the eighth, home.

As he neared his village he noticed that the big wood near his father's house seemed very small. Then, when he got to the village he thought he must be mad, for in the few days that he had been away the village had grown bigger, and the windmill had gone.

"What's become of the mill?" he asked a crowd of people. The boys and girls and men and women stared, then a very old man stepped fowards.

"It were pulled down," he said, "when I were a boy."

"And the woodcutter's cottage?"

"That were burned down fifty years ago.
Were you a native of these parts, old man?"

There was a large shop-window just
opposite and Diggory suddenly saw his
reflection in it – an old, old, white-haired
man on a white horse. He had a white
beard, too.

He almost tumbled off Invicta. The old man who had told him about the mill came and spoke to him, and poor old Diggory asked questions about all the people he knew and loved till he grew tired of hearing the answer, which was always the same, "Dead… dead… dead!"

Then he sat silent, and the people in the bar talked about his horses, and a young man said, "I wish I'd got just one of them. I'd set myself up in business, so I would."

"Young man," said Diggory, "you may take one, its name is Invicta."

The young man could hardly believe his ears. Diggory felt his heart warm to think that he had made someone else so happy. He actually felt younger. The very next morning he made up his mind to give away all the horses but one.

He led his horses away next day and gave away one in each village he passed through – and with every horse he gave away he felt happier and lighter. And when he had given away the fourth, his aches and pains went, and when he had given away the seventh his beard was gone.

"Now," he said to himself, "I will ride home and end my days in my own village."

So he turned his horse's head towards home, and he felt so much happier and fitter he could hardly believe that he was really an old, old man.

He rode on and when he reached the end of his village he stopped and rubbed his

eyes, for there stood the windmill and there was Joyce, looking prettier than ever.

"Oh, Diggory," she cried, "you've come back. Will you take me with you now?"

"Have you got a looking-glass?" he said. "Run and fetch it."

She brought it quickly and he looked in it, and he saw he was not old any more!

"Will you take me with you?" said Joyce.

He stooped down and kissed her sweet, pretty face.

"Of course," said he.

And as they went along to his home he told her the story.

"Well," she said, "you've got one wish-apple left."

"Why, so I have," said he.

"We'll make that into the fortune you went out to find," clever Joyce said.

And Diggory carried Joyce on Invicta to his father's house.

"You're soon back, my son," said the woodcutter, laughing.

"Yes," said Diggory.

"Have you found your fortune?"

"Yes," said Diggory, "here she is!"

"Well, well!" the woodcutter said, laughing more than ever.

So they were married, and they used the last wish-apple to set themselves up on a little farm. Diggory, Joyce and the white horse worked hard on the farm, so that they all prospered and were very happy as long as ever they lived.

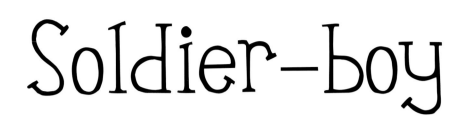

Soldier-boy

From *A Horse's Tale* by Mark Twain

Buffalo Bill was the nickname of American soldier and bison hunter William Frederick Cody, who lived through the last days of the Wild West, from 1846 to 1917. He was awarded the Medal of Honour for his services to the US army as a scout and later became famous for organizing shows with cowboy themes, which he toured around the United States, Europe and Great Britain.

I AM BUFFALO BILL'S HORSE. I have spent my life under his saddle – with him in it, too, and he is two hundred pounds, without his clothes, and there is no telling how much he weighs when he is out on the warpath and has his ammunition belted on.

He is young, over six feet, hasn't an

ounce of waste flesh, is straight, graceful, and nimble – quick as a cat. He has a handsome face and black hair dangling down on his shoulders and is beautiful to look at, and nobody is braver than he is, and nobody is stronger, except myself.

Yes, a person that doubts that he is fine to see should see him in his beaded buckskins, on my back and his rifle peeping above his shoulder, chasing an enemy, with me going like the wind and his hair streaming out behind him. Yes, he surely is a sight to look at then – and I'm part of it myself.

I am his favourite horse, out of dozens. I am not large but, big as he is, I have carried him thousands and thousands of miles on scout duty for the army. There's not a gorge, nor a pass, nor a valley, nor a fort, nor a trading post, nor a buffalo-range in the whole sweep of the Rocky Mountains and the Great Plains that we don't know as well as we know the bugle-calls. He is Chief of Scouts to the Army of the Frontier, and it makes us very important.

In such a position as I hold in the military service one needs to be of good family and be much better educated than most. Well, everybody says that I am the best-educated horse this side of the Atlantic, and the best-mannered. It may be so, it is not for me to say, modesty is the best policy, I think.

Buffalo Bill taught me the most of what

I know, my mother taught me some, and then I taught myself the rest. Lay a row of moccasins before me and I can tell you which tribe it comes from just by looking at it – Pawnee, Sioux, Shoshone, Cheyenne, Blackfoot, and as many other tribes as you please… name them in horse-talk that is, and I could do it in American if I had the means to speak aloud.

I know some of the Indian signs – the signs they make with their hands and by signal-fires at night and columns of smoke by day. Buffalo Bill taught me how to drag wounded soldiers out of the line of fire with my teeth, and I've done it, too – at least I've dragged him out of the battle when he was wounded. And not just once, but twice.

Yes, I know a lot of things. I remember bodies and faces and the way people walk, and if anyone ever shows me kindness I'll remember them forever.

I know the art of searching for a trail and I know the stale track from the fresh. I can keep a trail all by myself, with Buffalo Bill asleep in the

saddle – just ask him and he will tell you so. Many a time, when he has ridden all night, he has said to me at dawn, "Take the watch, Boy, if the trail freshens, call me."

Then he goes to sleep. He knows he can trust me, because I have an excellent reputation and have never let him down.

Now, I'll tell you a bit about my background. My mother was all American – she was of the best blood of Kentucky, the bluest Blue-grass aristocracy, and very proud. She spent her military life as the Colonel of the Tenth Dragoons, and saw a great deal of distinguished service. I mean, she carried the Colonel, but it's all the same. After all, where would he be without his horse? He simply wouldn't arrive – it takes two to make a colonel of dragoons.

My mother was a fine dragoon horse, but she never got above that. She was strong enough for the scout service, and had the endurance too, but she couldn't quite come up to the speed required – a scout horse has to have steel in his muscle and lightning in his blood.

My father on the other hand was a bronco, as wild as they come. When Professor Marsh was out here hunting bones for Yale University he found skeletons of horses no bigger than a fox, bedded in the rocks, and he said they were ancestors of my father – two million years old!

Professor Marsh said those skeletons were fossils. So that makes me part blue grass and

part fossil, if there is any older or better stock, I'd like to know about it.

And now we are back at Fort Paxton once more, after a forty-day scout, away up as far as the Big Horn river. Everything quiet. Crows and Blackfeet squabbling – as usual – but no outbreaks, and so the settlers are feeling fairly easy.

The Seventh Cavalry is still in garrison, here, as are the Ninth Dragoons, two artillery companies, and some infantry. They are all mighty glad to see me, including General Alison, the commandant.

The officers' ladies and children are very friendly. They call by to see me – and bring sugar with them. It was Tommy Drake and Fanny Marsh that remembered the sugar

this time. They are nice children, the nicest
at the post, I think. I know all about
children, and they adore me. Buffalo Bill
will tell you so himself.